paper thorn tree

hyena caves

crocodile river

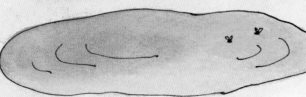

mud-bath

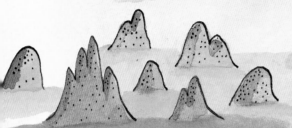

valley of 1000 anthills

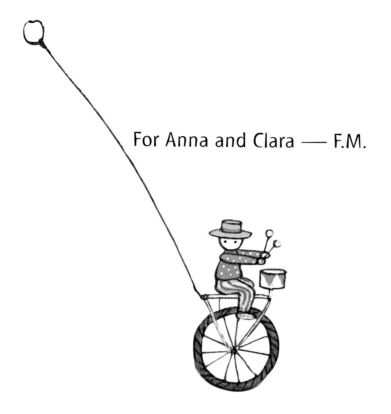

For Anna and Clara — F.M.

Noko and the Night Monster copyright © Frances Lincoln Limited 2001
Text and illustrations copyright © Fiona Moodie 2001

First published in Great Britain in 2001 by Frances Lincoln Limited
First American Edition

Marshall Cavendish
99 White Plains Road
Tarrytown, New York 10591

Library of Congress Cataloging-in-Publication Data

Moodie, Fiona.
Noko and the night monster / Fiona Moodie.
p. cm.
Summary: Takadu the aardvark comes up with an ingenious plan to help his friend Noko the porcupine overcome his fear of the night monster.
ISBN 0-7614-5093-9
[1. Monsters--Fiction. 2. Aardvark--Fiction. 3. Porcupines--Fiction. 4. Fear--Fiction.] I. Title.
PZ7.M7724 No 2001   [E]--dc21   00-060376

Printed in Singapore

1 3 5 6 4 2

Noko and the Night Monster

Fiona Moodie

MARSHALL CAVENDISH

NEW YORK

Takadu the aardvark and Noko the porcupine were old friends. They lived in a little house at the foot of the Mbombo hills. They had to work hard for a living but there was always time for fun.

Every evening, Noko
cooked soup for
dinner. As he worked,
Takadu would sing
a song to make it
cook faster:

O, lovely pot, shu shu shu,
It's surely not, shu shu shu,
Too much to ask, shu shu shu,
To boil our soup, shu shu shu,
And do it fast, shu shu shu.

   Noko's soup was
D E L I C I O U S !

But as soon as it got dark, Takadu said he was afraid of the Night Monster. Every bedtime it was the same. Takadu would shiver and shake, and Noko would read the wool prices from the *Farmer's Weekly* until he fell asleep.

In the morning Takadu always forgot how frightened he'd been the night before, and he would play his guitar, or talk to the dung beetles, or take the drum man for a walk. But Noko didn't forget. Noko was getting tired of reading the wool prices every night.

"What is this Night Monster anyway?" asked Noko, one morning. "Why don't you draw him for me so I'll know what he looks like?"

While Noko made clay pots, Takadu spent the morning trying to draw the Night Monster.

"That's him — that's the Night Monster," said Takadu at last.

And this is what he had drawn:

Next day, Noko got up early and crept out of the hut, taking Takadu's Night Monster picture with him. He left a message for Takadu:

Gone foraging. Back this evening. Soup in pot. Noko

First he went to see Mrs. Warthog in her mud-bath.

He showed her Takadu's picture and explained what
he wanted to do. Mrs. Warthog snorted with laughter.
"Of course I'll come," she said. "Mr. Warthog can babysit
for a change. I'll see you when the moon is full!"

Noko found Pangolin at the river. He showed him the picture and told him what he wanted him to do.

"Won't Takadu be upset, though?" asked Pangolin.

"Well," admitted Noko, "he might be at first. But I think it'll be worth it in the end."

Pangolin smiled a shy, slow, Pangolin smile.

"All right then," he said. "I'll join you at full moon."

It was nearly dark when Noko came across Hyena.

Hyena shook with giggles when Noko showed him the picture.

"Hee hee hee!" he guffawed. "What a brilliant idea! You can count on me, Noko — I can't wait for full moon."

Stars had begun to shine in the evening sky by the time Noko got home. Takadu was very glad to see him.

"You've been away all day," he snuffled, "and the soup's cold and I've made up a new song but it's really, really sad."

"I'm sorry, Takadu," said Noko. "Why don't I make us some fresh, hot soup?"

As Noko cooked, Takadu sang his new song and he felt much better. Then they went off to bed, and Noko read the wool prices until Takadu fell sleep.

A week later it was the night of the full moon.
Noko said he had to go out and take his sick
cousin some medicine.

Takadu was very frightened. He would have to
go to sleep without the wool prices, and what
about the Night Monster?

All at once, Takadu heard Noko's voice calling from far away.
"Takadu, Takadu!" and then again, "Takadu! Takadu!"

"I'll have to find Noko," Takadu said to himself. "I'll take the
broom to beat the Night Monster, and I must find Noko."
Takadu shivered and shook, but he tiptoed out.

Where was Noko's voice coming from?
   Takadu approached the rocks. They seemed even
bigger tonight. And what was that behind them?

It was the **Night Monster!**
Takadu didn't jump. He didn't scream. He shook
from his head to his toes, but he didn't run away.

Noko's voice came from behind the rock.

"Takadu! Takadu! Hurry up!"
Takadu charged right at the Night Monster and he
beat it **WHACK!** with the broom, right in its middle.

The most amazing thing happened.

The Night Monster came apart!
Takadu got such a fright that he fell on his back,
and Noko popped up, quite unharmed, from behind a rock.

Takadu was furious.

"That was a really HORRIBLE thing to do, Noko," he snorted. "I thought you were in danger. You made a fool of me and now I'm ANGRY!"

"But Takadu, you were so brave!" said Noko. "I called you and you came to find me in the dark! You whacked the Night Monster! You beat the Night Monster! No more Night Monster! Takadu, you're BRAVE!"

Takadu started to laugh.

"All right, Noko, I forgive you. At least I'll never be afraid of the Night Monster again."

"Thanks, Takadu," said Noko. "And now, let's have a party!"

So all the animals went back to the
hut and ate lots of sweetcorn and
drank lots of marula berry juice,
and when the sun came up,
they were still singing and dancing.

Now the party has begun,
Let's jump and jive, we'll have some fun.
Night Monster is no more,
Takadu kicked him out the door.
We are the friends who dance and sing,
We're not afraid of ANYTHING!